LEGENDS OF WILLIAM'S POINT

M.D. MARTIN

ISBN: 0-9990019-1-4
ISBN-13: 978-0-999019-1-2

This book is dedicated to my mom and
dad for believing in me and supporting my
writing decisions.

Legends of William's Point

Author's Note

William's Point was born in 1995 while I was attending Virginia Highlands Community College. I was surrounded by very talented, creative individuals and formed many lifelong friends that I consider part of my extended family. The first story in this novel - The Hybrid - is the first William's Point story I penned.

The idea was born on a warm autumn day when one of my close friends and I took a road trip to see some of the local out of the way sites I had never had the pleasure of visiting. After a day of site seeing we found ourselves in a small family restaurant with river rock floors and highly polished plank top tables.

It was in this atmosphere that the seeds of William's Point were planted in my mind. That evening when I went home, I sat down and began my journey by writing about Storm Matthews and his questioning of his existence. Since that day I haven't stopped exploring William's Point and all the characters that inhabit the small rural community set in the Blue Ridge Mountains.

I hope you enjoy your visit to the sleepy town where the monsters aren't always who you think and there is a fine line between light and dark.

TABLE OF CONTENTS

Welcome to William's Point. It's a small town and there really isn't much to look at but we seem to enjoy it here. Every summer we get bus loads, of blue haired tourists with their flash bulbs and endless rolls of budget film so they can remember what a quaint small town this is.

They like to sit on the verandas of my most famous land mark. A rambling one hundred room plantation house that used to belong to General George Armand, one of the lesser known Generals I assure you, but obscurity does not dissuade them. They flock to it like a smorgasbord. The plantation house was used to teach young girls how to become proper ladies then became a cat house for a time. Those were the dark years when my faithful parishioners were turning from me and I was a Shepard without a flock.

All traces of the cat house are gone now and the lost sheep returned to the fold after the tragedy. It was Satan's work, he had sent his minions among us and we had prevailed after the dark hour.

Those days are behind us now, no longer tarnishing our pristine reputation. The Armand house sits in stately splendor, a refuge to the weary traveler foolish enough to pay the exorbitant fees for lodging. Ah, but a fool and his money are soon parted.

My manicured lawns and crisp white picket fences line the nostalgic cobblestone streets and the deep awning shaded store fronts. Patchwork quilts of bright poppies and marigold are interspersed with slender irises and flowing orchids decorating the planters and borders of my developed persona. I am the spirit of small town Americana with children riding bicycles and carrying sparklers on the fourth of July. I am baseball and apple pie with a stagnant blackened blood that runs beneath my surface.

I hide my backwoods dusty faced miscreants and their quiet superstitions. My faults are wrapped in a thin veil of kindness, of neighborly concern and I lie to you with my superfluous charm and southern grace. I keep my secrets in my dense forests and hollows far from the light of your reasoning where my terrors will squeeze the life from you. I have given these places to *my* children, the ones no one can understand, and the ones no one will look upon. I listen to the others in this dark place, the ones that are *unnatural*. They are not of my blood but I love them as if they were my own. I fear them; I respect them.

These creatures of the night with their beautiful tragic fallen angel faces and glistening fangs that take only what they need. Creatures of the wilds, they live in the shadows save for some that are not afraid of what they truly are. They do not fear death instead they stalk it, they are freedom.

Already I hear their silent whispers echoing on the warm wind of encroaching darkness and I know that the time has come for me to bid you ado. It has been such a long time since I have heard their promising sighs and now I think I shall give in to their seduction and allow

them to come into my own heart.   Why not?   I
am, after all, a child of blood myself, born into it
from the first day man sat foot upon me.

THE HYBRID

Have you ever tasted blood? I mean really tasted blood. Have you ever had a hunger so insatiable or a thirst so unquenchable that no amount of food or wine could fulfill it? Blood, the ruby nectar of life that is so precious to so many. It is a rare commodity to find the purest of the pure and a treasure that I value with my life.

Now before you think I am a vampire because of my appetites I must tell you that I do not belong to that illustrious sect, regretfully. I belong neither to the immortals or the normal living beings, the ones that crawl along the freeways in their chrome and glass sarcophagi. I belong to a group consisting mainly of myself. I am sure that there are others like me but I am unaware of them at this time.

I am in turn savage and gentle. I have been called evil by those that are narrow minded and do not understand me or my existence. I have been viewed as a scientific miracle and monstrosity by educated men and women. I have been ostracized by my family since the tender age of four when my mother and father first realized that I was different.

Instead of playing with other children I stayed to myself and became obsessed with the basic rules of nature between the hunter and the hunted. I often wandered off into the woods behind our house and watched for hours on end as snakes swallowed small field mice and the spiders crawled on their nimble legs toward the trapped and panicking flies that were silly enough to stumble into their sticky lair.

To look at me you wouldn't know of my, shall we say, unusual appetites. You could pass me in a store, the school hallway, on the street and never know who I am. I could be your best friend, your neighbor, your lover. Your lover. I have never denied my passion for the opposite sex. I worship women, I adore women, I am obsessed with them. I love their softness, their essence, their sensuality. Most men take them for granted or simply ignore the mystery that surrounds the soft vixens that haunt their most erotic dreams. Not I.

Women, since the age of fifteen I have been captivated by them. I have loved them with a fierce abandon that amazed even me. I have also been obsessed with one. Do you know what it's like to become so impassioned with one person that all sense of right and wrong are suspended and one thought burns like a fever in your blood?

I am not one of those men that they do a movie of the week about. I do not stalk young women and frighten them to death. I have always prided myself on being better than those poor fools that can't seem to tell fact from fiction. No, I do not stalk women. I love them too much for that. My blood has made a very insatiable man, the flesh is weak.

I stare blankly at this monitor, not sure why I am writing this for everyone to read. I'm sure many of you will judge me but that is nothing new. Madness, isn't that what most great tragedies are based on? The poor characters that stroll across the stage are truly mad in their own rights.

Each person must deal with his own demons; his own madness, but most just sit quietly while it slowly eats them alive. I on the other hand, am Madness personified. I am a genetic what-if that never should have been. My dear sweet, angelic mother and my father didn't know that inside each of them, they carried the one dormant gene that would create the creature they gave birth to. I remember going to church on Sundays, sitting beside my mother on the front pew and listening to my father preach his sermons.

He talked of sin and the serpent in the garden and of man's downfall. Then he talked of the evil that Satan wrought when he led man astray, of the evil that the devil could plant in the seed of an unborn child because of the faithlessness of two married people. He preached long and hard of the weakness of the flesh and of temptation. He stared at me the whole time and I knew what he was saying, he was denouncing me in front of the whole congregation. He was telling everyone that my dear sweet mother was less than what she had always been to me.

Then came the tests. My father contacted some of the doctors he had known when he had been an intern.

Tests. What a waste of a word. Torture would be more suitable. Blood was a favorite of theirs and they couldn't seem to get enough of mine. Four times a day they would take my blood; you know after a while the needles cease to hurt. I was put under glass you could say, I was studied twenty-four hours a day. While I slept they watched me; when I woke they watched me; when I ate they studied me.

For fourteen long years they probed me, they poked me, they turned me every which way they could and probably would have loved to cut me open save for the fact that I was a living, breathing 'human'. All the time my hunger was growing to a fever pitch and I knew that it was going to surpass even my control.

It was the eve of my eighteenth birthday when I awoke with the worst gnawing in my stomach I had ever felt. My body trembled as I staggered from my hospital bed and made my way into the tiny cubicle of a bathroom. The fluorescent's blinded my sensitive eyes as I splashed icy water in my face and fought down the wave of nausea.

I felt like a man that had been starved and my throat burned with thirst. A thirst I had never known. It was a thirst for something more substantial than the chilly water that cascaded over my open palms. I needed food.

I pressed the call button and slipped into a primal crouch on the floor, instinctively taking up this ageless predatorial stance. The orderly that came to my room was accompanied by another burlier man that had been working at the hospital for four months now. I don't know what his name was but I rarely ever worry about names anymore.

They pushed the door open and found me crouched there. I must have been a terrifying sight with my eyes glazed over with the blood lust that creeps into them. I have seen it myself many times. I launched myself at them like a man possessed and quite possibly I was. The need for sustenance overrode any fear that I might have had that they could take me. Instead I went for the throat on first one man and then I lunged for the other as he tried to run from the room. I'm sure their screams were heard in the hallway but since it was so late at night there weren't many on duty in this ward at least.

I didn't care. I was in such a fever, I think I would have taken all them on. The first taste is always the most bitterly sweet. Salty with just a touch of metal. Nourishment. Fulfillment. Something to quench the burning thirst and quiet my stomach. I ate.

Sometime later, after the fever pitch had left my body I realized what I had done. I wept as I stared at the two lifeless bodies that were now surrounded by the crimson pool of their own life's essence. It slowly slipped from the torn flesh to run in ruby rivers to the pristine white floor. Everything is so harsh in the light, but in the shadows, there are areas that seem less real. Not so with this. The light was harsh, it clearly outlined the dead men lying on the floor and it clearly showed me covered with their blood, smeared across my mouth, dripping from my hands, coating the front of my sweat pants.

Time; it can play tricks on the mind. Something may seem to take forever when in all actuality in only takes a few seconds. I felt like I had stared at those bodies for days but I had only stood there for two minutes before I realized that I had to get out of there. I had to run, to get away before others came and put me in those awful padded cells with the jacket again. I grabbed the items closest to me and ran out the door, unmindful of the bloody footprints I left in my wake.

***

I fled from the hospital, into the shroud of glorious night. I never looked back, I never thought about that place again until just now. I guess we all have demons that we need to exorcize every now and again and I guess that's what I had to do. I escaped to the city, the crowds of nameless faces that blend together in a melting pot providing me with the cover I needed to stay out of the reach of the authorities. I made my home among the homeless, the street people.

I started there but I worked my way up. I rose from the masses to become what I am today. I knew that I ran a risk of being caught by the doctors, the law. I knew I could be tried for the murder of the two orderlies but life has a funny kind of twist to it when you're poor.

It was like looking through a warped

window pane, those with money could do anything but those without it only dreamed of getting it. I had my reasons for wanting money, none of which had anything to do with luxury. More of my need for the root of all evil were the demands of my hunger.

The depth of my obsession with women drove me to do things that I wouldn't have ever thought of were I a normal person. But as I have already said, I am anything but normal, I can take pride in my differences as gruesome as they sound to you.

I was on my own for the first time in my life, without nurses or doctors to monitor me every minute of the day. I admit that I wasn't ready for the world due to my imprisonment in the hospital. I felt like a kid let loose in a candy store. There were so many things to do, so many tastes to indulge, and so many pleasures to experience. My lust for blood was running like wildfire through my body and every night I prowled the city streets searching for my next meal.

That first month of freedom I fed every night twice, sometimes three times. My body was famished from the denial of eighteen long years. I couldn't contain the hunger that sang through my veins and I didn't want to. I loved the feedings, they were the only time I felt truly alive. The thrill of stalking my victim, of luring them into a darkened alley or a blind street. I didn't care.

Once I crept onto a fire escape and waited while the couple inside parted for the evening then I slipped inside for a midnight snack. The bodies were never found. I am extremely immaculate about the disposal of my meals. No need to cause city-wide panic over a few dead bodies. No need to leave a trail for the authorities to follow either.

I took to the nightlife like a fish to water and it wasn't long before I knew everyone on the streets. I knew the junkies, the whores, the runaways. I was every one of them in a sense, and yet I was none of them. I was always different, and I learned that different was better.

It was one of my nights out that I met a man by the name of Randolph. He was rather temperamental in his moods and I soon found that he had alternative tastes which I did not share. He never made an advance on me, however, so I paid little attention to his private indulgences.

Randolph was a manager of sorts. He handled many of the actors and actresses of the silver screen. He also managed bands, models, and clothing lines. He was interested in my looks, my healthy glow. I soon became a model for one of the clothing firms he had as a client. It was an easy job for good money and they asked very little about my private life.

At first, I was worried that I would be detected quickly by the agents that dogged my tracks but I learned that Randolph could help with anything. I changed my name, grew my hair long and took on another personality. He falsified my birth record and found out some things from my past that I wanted to know.

Through it all he only smiled and looked the other way. His percentage was handsome enough to blind him.

It was during my shot in Milan that I met Alexis, my first obsession. She was an olive-skinned beauty with dark, brandy brown eyes that beckoned me to stay with her. Her hair was a long dark waterfall that made my hands ache to touch it.

During our affair, I fed less but I still felt as if something was missing. Alexis was a goddess but she was shallow. She loved to be told that her beauty surpassed the sun but she was fickle when she was behind closed doors. Public displays were more her forte. I, on the other hand, am a private person. I want to keep my business behind a veil, not on display for everyone to see.

I moved on from Alexis to being a single man again, during which time my feeding resumed with an exaggerated level of ferocity. I wanted to eat at odd times during the day as well as the night and I found that it nearly exhausted me to keep up with my appetite. Randolph suggested that I take a vacation to relax and get my head straight before I became careless. I agreed.

It was during that summer that I met her. Eve was my obsession. She was my passion. She was my downfall. How ironic that I would choose a woman who followed in the footsteps of her namesake. Maybe something from my father's hellfire brimstone sermons had stuck with me. Maybe original sin was a great intoxication that wooed my wild soul and seduced me into the recklessness with which I pursued the woman. Whatever the reason, I knew that I had to have her or die from the denial.

Lust is a driving emotion. It rules the body and soul when it takes hold. It was almost as strong as my hunger and the two warred with each other constantly, driving me to the razors edge of madness.

Have you ever experienced the need to possess another living being? I don't mean in an ownership capacity, I mean to own their heart, their mind. Have you ever wanted to be the one and only thought that lurks in their mind from sun up till the next morning? Have you ever been consumed by the indescribable lust that would make you want to commit murder to have what your heart desired most?

Murder. The word has a jagged past and yet most people feel that just my existence proves their theories about murder to be correct. Am I a murderer because I feed from the human body, the blood? Are you a murderer if you feed from the flesh of an animal? It's a double-edged sword, isn't it? Yes, murder is a complex word that has a depth of meanings and hidden agendas.

Eve was my serpent. She was a married woman that had all the allure of Helen of Troy. Men threw themselves at her feet and I was included in that set. I shamelessly allowed her to use me in the hopes that I could breach the walls she had built around her heart. Walls that held everyone out, walls that her husband had put there. Barbed wire could never be as prickly as Eve or as effective at keeping one out. I was determined and determination if wielded properly, can be a powerful thing.

It was on a balmy, sea swept night that I met Eve. I walked alone through the cobblestone streets of a small town on the eastern seaboard. Temperatures had been reaching record breaking highs during the months of May and June; and July was proving to be no different. I had arrived only a few days before and had just gotten settled into one of the many condominiums that Randolph owned. I had become acquainted with some of Randolph's friends in the complex and was happy to have a few moments alone.

I smiled at the whimsy of the cobblestone street, now all I needed was a dense fog to roll in to complete the mood. My sense of humor has always been as morbid as my fascinations. I strode to the railing of the boardwalk just off the street and stood staring out at the glistening ocean as she rolled her body sensuously against the sandy shoreline. It was on this breeze that I smelled her, that slow burning woman scent that made my lips curl in a feral wanting. I could almost taste her on my lips and before I ever saw her, I knew that I had to have her.

Eve was a woman with a wanton's desires and I could feel them as they ran rampant through her body. She was strolling along the beach with her long dark hair hanging loose to catch the wind and whip out behind her. Her slight figure made a beautiful contrast to the wide expanse of the sea and horizon. The billowing white skirt she wore caught in the trade winds and blew up around her knees, exposing the slender curves of her thighs and calves.

In that moment, I knew a lust stronger than my hunger could have ever been and I felt myself being propelled over the railing and landing squarely on the powdery sand. I was not a man but more of an animal and Eve was my prey. I stalked down the beach, watching for even the slightest glimpse of flesh as the breeze continued to play with her skirt. I longed to grab hold of that flimsy cloth and rip if from her body, to lay her in the sand and show her what real passion was, but I didn't. I followed instead like some wild creature follows that which it does not understand but yearns to touch, to feel, to be felt. I tracked through the sand, obliterating her delicate footprints with my own and taking savage pride in taking her steps.

Eroticism can be gained in many ways, for some a simple foot massage may do it. The forms of pleasure depend upon the person feeling it and as I sit here and write this, I swear to you that with each step I took that had once belonged to her, it was as if I buried myself deeper into her woman's heart. This may sound strange to you, it would to me if I hadn't felt it with every fiber of my soul. For once the hunger was silent, but in its place another hunger had just begun to rage and I knew that to feed this hunger would be to destroy her or myself: or both.

We traveled up the beach and I knew that she was aware of every step I took, every breath I breathed, ever agonizing second, I spent trying to catch another glimpse of her body. She turned when she came to the wooden steps leading up to her beachfront cottage and smiled a slow seductive smile at me. Her eyes held all the promises of the days to come and I felt myself swell at the thought. Soon, she told me silently, soon I will come to you and we will be as one. Then you will be mine and then your hell will begin. And so, it did.

It had been a week since I had first seen Eve with her swaying skirts and legs with their promised Eden nestled between their thighs. I had fed off and on as usual but with a decided lack of enthusiasm as my mind had continued to wander back to those few seconds of shared intellect. They say the greatest pleasure center we have in our bodies is the mind, I would have disagreed before I met her but not anymore. A mere thought of a person can almost bring some to climax and Eve was of the same ilk I am sure.

I stood on the balcony of the condominium, listening to Jarred and Michael bicker about some minute point they were trying to make. I only half listened to the pair, I had grown tired of their ceaseless arguments after the first day. They had both at one time or another been one of Randolph's lovers and their favorite pastime seemed to be to compare stories of the old days. I was less than interested.

I sipped the rum and coke that I had brought with me from the kitchen and listened to one of the bands that was playing farther down the boardwalk at a club that I had visited many times. Their wild beat fed its way into my blood and set the rhythm for my mood. My blood stirred and I knew that I would become restless before long. It was then that I smelled her again, the haunting melody of her femininity. My sable brow arched high above my black as sin eyes and I vaulted over the railing to land solidly on the sand below.

I heard the gasps of the two I had just left behind but they rarely questioned my abilities due to some attraction they had. I assure you it was not returned. I strode down the beach in the direction of that scent and I felt my loins tighten as I came nearer to its source. I could hear her just beyond the rock outcropping that spilled into the sea. Her soft husky voice was raised in panic and I was spurred on to race up across the treacherous rocks and find the source of her fear.

The scene that stretched out below me sent my blood rushing through my ears and I felt the first edges of the yawning black abyss inside myself that I had never known before. He towered above her as she lay on the beach, helpless to his power as he glared down at her. Words passed his lips in a hiss no mortal man could have heard unless he had been right up on them but I heard them. Hate and contempt dripped from his lips as he bent to take what she didn't want to offer and I sprinted down the beach aware of the rushing wind in my ears and the stifled screams coming from her throat.

I was on them in a matter of seconds and before I was aware of what I was doing, I had the man in my arms and was sinking my teeth into his throat as he struggled against me. I took pleasure in making it hurt, I could have been gentle but he hadn't been. I drained him and then licked at my bloodied hands when I let him drop on the sand. I stared with hate and disgust at his dead white body as the tide swept up to caress his face. I couldn't contain what I did next as I leaned over him and spit some of his own blood back onto his cold face. Too bad I hadn't made it last longer but the anger had taken hold and I had been like a sail being buffeted by a large wind.

"You killed him." she whispered from behind me.

I tensed, having forgotten her presence. She had seen me feed and now she would surely curse me and try to summon help. I couldn't allow that but I couldn't bring myself to kill her either. My back stiffened as I readied myself to face her. When I did, I was surprised at what I found. Her eyes held no condemnation, instead they were glazed as if she were drunk but I couldn't detect any alcohol on her.

"You killed him." she murmured again as she took a step back from me.

I knew what would happen, was tensed and ready for it.

"We have to get rid of the body. Quick, bring him to the house. Come on before someone else come running because they heard me screaming." she led the way, all quiet grace and dignity in her torn clothing and disarrayed hair.

I was proud of her ability to think in the grip of the terror I still felt hiding inside her. I picked up the dead body and followed her up the wooden stairs into the beach front cottage. We made our way through the huge gathering room to the stainless-steel kitchen and I laid him on the counter indicated in passing.

"Here, I'm not strong enough to cut through bone but you are. I will take care of the rest." she said as she handed me a cleaver then went to the pantry to rummage about for a meat press.

I felt nausea as I watched the methodical way she worked at the pieces I cut from him. Not once did she flinch when she ground the meat up into something akin to hamburger, mixing real beef with that of the dead man. I had never been involved in something as twisted as this and I wondered if I hadn't stepped into one of my own nightmares.

We worked through the night and by morning had finished him off. I stood by the railing of the back veranda taking in the fresh scent of the sea and letting it wash the lingering odor of death from my nostrils. My hands were clean but they still felt dirty from my nighttime activities. I felt her presence behind me but did not turn.

"Do you hate me now?" she asked as she pressed her soft breasts against my back.

"No, I cannot hate you for something I did." I replied but still did not turn to face her.

"Then face me and tell me that you still want me. Tell me that what I have made you do did not turn your stomach and make you wish you had never seen me.   Tell me that you haven't changed your mind." she pressed herself closer to me and my blood stirred again as her scent filled my being with lust.

"Of course, I haven't changed my mind." I mumbled as I pulled her around in front of me so that she could see the sun rise.

Burnished gold streaked the sky and lit in her dark hair as it fluttered around us in a halo of wicked proportions and fell across my muscular biceps urging me to take what my victory had given me.   She was mine now and I was her slave to command, she knew it as well as I.   She had seen me feed and now my life was in her hands to do with what she would because I could no more kill her than myself.

"Tonight, you will come to the party that Frank was going to throw and you will be welcomed into the midst of the party goers and as they dine we will sit back and enjoy our silent laughter. They will never know that they are consuming his death and neither will the police. I will tend to the bones, for now I want you to rest then after the party and we have discovered that Frank is missing you will be the good friend that Frank always talked about.   The friend that will console his widow and then we will have the rest of our lives to do as we wish.   Do you understand?" she raised a dark brow as she stared into my eyes.

Her hands were so small as they pressed to the sides of my face and held me still while she implored me with her dark gaze to continue the charade for her guests. I nodded and began to realize just how much power she would have over me. I didn't know if I was going to be free or helpless, at any rate I was hers to do with as she pleased and I was the one that had delivered myself unto her. The torment was just beginning.

The party was a success and I had to admit that Eve was the consummate actress, imploring her quests of Frank's whereabouts. She worried and wrung her hands when the dining room was prepared and Frank still had not come home. She accepted the gentle pats and comforting words from her friends and smiled forlornly as if she were truly worried for his wellbeing.

I was introduced around and even *remembered* by some of the quests as a gentleman that had accompanied Frank and Eve to the Caymans a few years ago or Bermuda last fall. I was sought out for legal advice because Frank had mentioned my business mind or leered at by the ladies because of my rake hell reputation that some of the other ladies had bragged about. In general, I became one of them and when the police were notified they defended me as one of their own.

"Who Storm? No, he and Frank have been together since college. He is only here to give Eve a comforting shoulder to cry on and why not, he's been there for her for years. No, Frank probably ran into the business end of a shotgun that belonged to a jealous husband. Frank was a notorious cheat and he was never faithful to his poor innocent wife. Eve was always there for him and never unfaithful. If it were up to me, she and Storm would be married tomorrow but I don't know if she will ever feel that way about Storm." they all said when the police interrogated them.

The days passed and still no word from the police as they searched for the missing Frank and still the crowd insisted that I was one of them. I was expected to take Franks place after the weeks had passed into a few months. Eve had held herself at bay all through this time, teasing me with the one thing I wanted above all and making me her puppet. I danced on her strings quite well and soon took over the company that Frank and I had shared. The board didn't object and I was now the head of a company I knew little or nothing about.

Before you ask how I could assume such a position without physical evidence of part ownership, I must tell you that Eve was persuasive with the board and just one look always seemed to get her what she wanted. I didn't make the decisions though, I was merely a figurehead for her corporation. In private, I found that Eve was ruthless and that if I made a move to leave her, she never failed to remind me of the deed I had done.

All the while she taunted me with her sensuous body then held me at bay with her cold words and barbed venom. I now know what real hell is and I had fallen into it without the least qualm. We were married six months after Frank's disappearance at his family's urging.

"Frank would want you to protect Eve, you were always the one he trusted the most." they had said.

His mother had pleaded with me to take care of the jewel of Frank's eye and I had buckled beneath the trust in the woman's pale, tear shimmering eyes. My stomach had lurched at the thought of life with this heartless bitch and I tell you now that if I could kill her I would. I have stood over her every night and stared at her quiet beauty, the delicate eyelids that hide the truth in some peaceful slumber known only to her and long to sink my teeth into her throat, to drain the life from her limbs and toss her into the ocean. To grind her up in the same meat press that she had used on Frank and serve her up to our friends for dinner but I cannot. I bend forward and feel the hot pulse of her blood as I press my mouth to her willing throat but I cannot sink my teeth in and finish the deed.

She torments me with her unwillingness to become my mistress and even in marriage I do not take her. My obsession has grown to hate and now I know why Frank acted as he did. He couldn't take anymore and had lashed out but I have never, nor will ever hurt a woman so I am doomed to this purgatory of my own folly. Maybe someday someone will save me from myself but until then I will live out my days as her puppet and dare not look at another for fear of my life. I am cursed just as my father once preached, I am sentenced to something far worse than drinking blood for nourishment. I have tasted blood and I have loved the pain of its bitter sweetness as it feeds my body but I am now a prisoner of my one true obsession.   May God have mercy on me.

CHARRED

Deacon Drake's footsteps were clumsy as he clamored across the slick lichen covered rocks lining the craggy shoreline of the unrelenting lake. His ragged breath thundered in his ears and reverberated in his chest. His lungs felt like they were on fire as he faltered, trying to find a place to hide amongst the now sliding shale slope he had stumbled on to. If only he could disappear, completely lose himself amongst the barren shoreline. The pitiless moon emerged from the dark cloud bank, her full bloody radiance bathing the landscape in scarlet. It was a hunter's moon and he was the hunted.

Deacon stopped and swallowed; the spittle burned his raw throat. Sweat trickled down his face and stained his shirt and trousers. He listened but there was no sound other than his own ragged breathing as his starved lungs fought for every ounce of oxygen they could get. His teeth gnashed as his head swiveled from side to side surveying the vaguely familiar surroundings. The hateful brilliance of the full harvest moon reflected from the water's surface. There were no waves, no ripples, no sign of life other than his own miniscule existence.

The sound of shifting shale sent Deacon whirling in a circle to survey the area again. A shower of the loose rock was dislodged by his imprudent movements and sent him falling. He bit back the sudden cry of pain and raised his hand to look at the fresh cuts from the sharp shards of broken rock. Blood trickled from the lacerations on his palm.

Through his spread fingers he could see the glassy surface of the lake. On the distant shore, a small glow ignited. Orbs of blue and green and white burnt across the mirror face of the lake. *Witches fire* his jumbled thoughts clattered. Instinctively he scrambled backwards crab clawing his way up the ever-shifting slope. Centuries of superstitious stories whispered through his mind.

Should he be more terrified of the strangely burning lights or his pursuers?

Deacon choked on a yelp of terror as his hand fell on a large furry object. A growl rumbled above him and reverberated through his fingers where they rested on the paw. His heart lurched in his chest. A long trail of saliva dribbled on to his shoulder and he dared not turn his head. He didn't want to consider those burning eyes or see the bloodstained teeth with their horrid black lips rolled back. The growl rumbled again and he felt his heart falter. A hysterical laugh threatened to bubble up in his throat. He was sure he had finally lost his senses.

I'm caught between the devil and the deep blue sea.

"Did you really think you could get away?" a deep voice rolled from the darkness to his left.

Deacon swallowed hard again, trying to push past the lump that had formed in his throat. He opened his mouth to speak but found his voice frozen with fear. He gulped like a fish starved for oxygen and shifted uneasily. The growl rumbled above him again and powerful jaws snapped by his ear.

"I wouldn't move if I were you. My brother didn't enjoy the chase you sent him on. Now, instead of letting you live, he may want some payback," the voice crooned as heated breath fanned the tiny hairs on the back of Deacon's neck.

The stench of decayed flesh and old blood mingled with the stink of his fear and sent an involuntary spasm into his throat. He turned his head to the right and heaved the last of his grandmother's chicken and gravy on to the cold uncaring shale.

A chuckle along with another rumbling growl filtered through Deacon's foggy brain and he knew they were both laughing at him. He glanced back out across the surface of the water and saw that the witches' lights had grown closer.

"Don't even think about it. They're too far away for you. Now, where is he?" an edge had crept in to the disembodied voice.

Deacon shook his head no and swiped at the snot and spittle that was left on his face. It may be too late for him but he wouldn't betray his family. He wouldn't tell the two monsters where they could find his cousin Caleb Whitewolf. He didn't know why they wanted Caleb but he would take the information to his grave.

"Don't be stupid! Don't think that we won't kill you right there," the voice snapped in annoyance.

"On the contrary," he managed to choke out, "that is exactly what I think you're going to do."

A string of curses the likes of which mankind had not heard uttered in centuries cut through the shadows as the figure finally emerged. The rage that coursed through the man was palpable. His eyes burned red in the gore of the moons rays. The left half of his face was burnt and scared almost melting before Deacon's eyes.

"Looks like you've been kissed by the Furies fire," Deacon dared to goad.

"Do I? Well look harder cousin because soon you'll be joining us," the man halted his erratic pacing and fixed him with an unwavering stare.

Deacon felt his will being sucked out through his belly button. It was the one true portal to your body and soul; that was what his grandmother had always told him. In a flash of foresight, he knew what they intended and cursed himself for a fool. He should have listened to his Granny and not invited trouble but the arrogance of youth was boundless. He should have stayed at home and finished the argument with Mina instead of taking the dare that the jocks had given him to go to the turntable this late at night.

No one ever went to the turntable and came back to tell about it. There were things back there in the depths of the woods, awful, horrible things that wanted much more than your soul. He had been a fool and now pride had landed him on to this slope at the edge of the lake with the devil's hellhound at his back and this burnt tormentor staring at him.   His attention was torn from the man's features when he noticed a disturbance coming from the water.

From the depths of the lake she emerged, a dark vengeful Goddess.   Her hair was as black as a raven's wing and her eyes were bottomless pools.   Eternity cloaked her in gossamer gowns of ebony as she glided towards the shore.   Her skin was as pale as cold dead flesh, her lips and fingertips as black as the darkest night.   Runic symbols adorned her barely concealed breasts. She was the embodiment of the evil that lived in every man's soul and she had come for his.

Black flames danced about her as she glided across the shale never disturbing a shard. Wind danced through her hair where there was no wind.   The world seemed dead, devoid of anything but her.

"Look in to her eyes, drown in their infinite depths.   Does she appeal to you *cousin*?   Does she . . . arouse you?" his tormentor's voice had grown husky.

Deacon fought to shake his head in denial but the will to move had been stolen from him.

"Don't lie.   She can taste your deceit. Would you like to know what her creamy breasts feel like?   How her lips would feel upon your undeserving skin that even now reeks of the weakness of humanity?   Maybe if you ask her nicely she will let you find out," the man squatted beside him casting an adoring gaze up at the deity before them.

A small smile traced across her full supple lips as she ensnared Deacon with her fathomless gaze.

"Too late cousin, you waited too long," the man tsked as he basked in the cold affection of her soulless stare.

There was a loud crack and Deacon felt as if someone had slammed their hand into his stomach and grabbed hold of his insides. His back bowed forward painfully as the invisible hand jerked hard, a jubilant smile spread across her beautiful face contorting her features as she contorted his body. His eyes blinked rapidly as she raised her hand triumphantly towards the heavens. There dangling from those blackened fingertips was a white wispy shroud of ethereal splendor. It pulsed and ebbed and deep down he knew what it was. Deacon's soul was writhing around on her hateful fingertips. Vaguely, he wondered how he could be alive when the very thing that made him human was no longer in his body.

"You can live without a soul cousin . . . *people* do it all the time. Count yourself lucky though, you're getting yours back . . . with a few minor adjustments," the man smiled as he poked at the vapor that held the mystery of mankind in its ebbing depths making Deacon long to throw up again.

The soul twitched and writhed in agony as it began to turn as ashy gray as a winter morn then begin to burn and curl at the edges. Just before it was charred beyond all comprehension she shoved it back into his body the searing pain worse than any Deacon had ever experienced in his brief life. Her throaty laughter split the silence of the night and somewhere in the distance he heard the baying of a hound then a flash of purple lightning graced the mountaintops.

"We'll be in touch *cousin*. Until then, enjoy your new lease on life," the man whispered hastily as they seemed to evaporate, slipping back in to the shadows from whence they came.

Deacon panted, overwhelmed by the ravenous hunger he now felt for a fresh soul to steal as the bloody moon hid her face behind a cloud and wept with glee.

THE HOUSE WHERE NO ONE LIVED

The savage wind tore at the tree tops, pressing them back towards the earth. The scent of rich dark soil and the approaching rain combined and stuck in the back of Mina's throat as she snuggled down in to her jacket. Leaves shuddered and fell as the limbs clattered like bare bones above her as she passed through the woods on her way to the cabin. She absently patted the note that lay nestled in her jeans pocket. She had been overjoyed to finally hear from Deacon again. He had disappeared almost a week ago with no word.

The last time they seen each other they had argued. He had asked her to run away with him and she had refused. She had regretted that decision but hoped that now she would have the chance to make it up to him. She knew that he had endured a lot of ridicule from the people of William's Point because of his family ties. They lived in a small town and no one had any secrets. Everyone knew that Deacon's cousin, Caleb Whitewolf, had been mixed up with the

Wynn's in the past and that was enough to put a mark on your own record.

The Wynn's, just the thought of that family sent a chill down her spine that even the fury of the storm couldn't match. Everyone in town knew all the Wynn's were witches; and they lived in mortal fear of them. She just hoped that Deacon hadn't gotten mixed up in all that business. Fear propelled her forward, quickening her step. She was anxious to see Deacon and assure herself that he was alright. He must be; he had sent her the message to meet him at their secret hideout.

Thoughts of the Wynn family and Caleb vanished as she entered the small clearing where the ancient hunting cabin sat decaying. There were no lights in the window, maybe she had arrived before Deacon. No matter, she could build a fire just as easily as he could. She rushed forward as the first fat drops of rain began to pelt angrily from the heavens.

She lurched through the old oak door mindful of the rotting logs and slick moss that lined the front porch. The rain crashed against the tin roof and setup a deafening tattoo that ate away at her thoughts. She pushed the door shut behind her and made sure the latch was set so the wind couldn't shove it open again.

The inside of the cabin was dark and dank, smelling of must and mildew. Shadows were as thick as soup and she could barely make out the dim outlines of the moldering furniture. The fireplace, she knew, was at the opposite end of the cabin. There would be kindling and tinder and logs laid for a fire; she and Deacon always made sure to leave it ready for their next rendezvous.

She knelt near the cold hearth and searched in the darkness for the pack of matches they kept near the coal shuttle. Her hand fell upon a furry object and she jerked back out of pure instinct. A high-pitched squeal sent her falling backwards as tiny clawed feet scuttled away from her. She shook her head in the darkness and almost laughed at her squeamishness.

It was just a rat, she thought as she moved back to the fireplace and found the matches.

There was a tiny pop as the match head blazed brilliantly, blinding her momentarily in the gloom. She set the match to the dry kindling and soon had a cozy fire started. Heat radiated from the hearth as the wood caught and the first smell of smoke mingled with the damp dankness of the old logs to make an almost homey combination. It was a familiar scent, one she relished and identified with long evenings spent in Deacon's arms watching the flames lick at the firewood.

She extended her frozen fingers to the heat of the fire and smiled as she thought of Deacon, surely, he would be along soon. The wind shifted and chuffed some of the smoke back down the chimney in to her face. Mina clapped a hand over her mouth as she began to cough and moved away from the now blazing fire. She wiped her eyes and face hoping there was no soot there, she wouldn't want to see him looking like a beggar. She went to the old wash stand and opened a bottle of water they had left behind and grabbed a wash cloth from the drawer to wipe her face clean.

Her movements were arrested by a scraping sound that was barely audible above the pounding of the rain overhead. She dropped the washcloth across the bar to dry and turned around to survey the cabin. Her heart froze in her chest when she found him squatted on the sagging mattress watching her with eyes almost too pale to be his.

Deacon's hair had grown considerably since she had last seen him. He was shaggy and unkempt and still wearing the same clothes he had worn when he disappeared from his grandmother's house. His fingers were filthy as if he had been grubbing in the dirt for something. She couldn't help the displeasure that snarled her lip. He presented a miserable picture and she wondered what he had been doing.

"Where have you been?" she asked as she approached him.

Deacon didn't answer or blink or move for that matter. He just stayed squatted on the old mattress watching her as she walked closer. He was beginning to frustrate her with his prolonged silence. Why wouldn't he answer or acknowledge her? What was the matter with him? She was on the verge of asking that very question when the hasp on the door gave way beneath the onslaught of a fresh bout of wind and blew open.

The storm rushed in, rain pelted her like stinging needles and the wind did its best to put out the fire she had started. She stopped midway in her trek to Deacon and turned to shove the door closed again. They were going to have to fix that hasp if they intended to keep meeting here, she thought. She tossed her blonde braid back over her shoulder and turned running directly in to his chest.

"Deacon!" she gasped as she fell back against the door.

His silence unnerved her as his dirty fingers reached out and fingers the fine hair of her gleaming braid. Deacon had always been quiet but this was different. She looked up at those pale blue eyes and felt a trickle of fear tiptoe down her spine. There was nothing behind those eyes. Nothing. It was as if she were looking at a house where no one lived. As the thought dawned on her that she shouldn't have come his hand twisted in her braid and yanked her back to him.

Terror seized her as she tried to yank her hair free, trapped between him and the door. He looped her braid around her neck once, twice, three times pulling it tighter each time. His face remained impassive. Mina coughed as she clawed at his hands then the ridged set of his jaw and finally at his eyes, anything to make his loosen his grip. She tried to scream but her air was cut off as he yanked again on the end of the braid. Darkness began to swirl up and engulf her as the cold chill crept into her fingers again.

Numb, she was so numb.   Then there was nothing.

THE GATEWAY

Blackened silhouettes of dead tree trunks pressed against the gloom of dusky evening as the dying light filtered through the murky shadows of twilight.   A chill wind swept through the silent trees as darkness descended.   Two figures slipped through the stand of old oaks, making their way toward the forbidden place locals called the turntable.   The hushed echoes of their foot falls were the only sounds that broke the cold silence of the gateway, the entrance to the turntable.   No one dared to venture back this far in the woods, no one wanted to.   The rumors of the evil that lived back in the mountains ran rampant through the folklore of the people of the region.   The stories were used mainly to scare the children but as with most folktales there is always a grain of truth hidden in its meaning.

"How much farther?" Erica asked as she moved quickly behind her companion.

"Not much farther, just keep your voice down.   We don't want to startle anything that might be sleepin'," Jobey whispered over his overall clad shoulder.

Erica stared at her country cousin, squinting to see through the growing darkness. A small smile slid across her lips as she followed him past two hulking monoliths of natural rock. She hadn't believed the stories that her cousins had told her when she arrived just a few short days ago. Erica was a city girl to the core and didn't believe in witches and ghosts, let alone the evil that was supposed to live in these woods. A giggle escaped her as she walked solemnly behind him.

"What are you gigglin' 'bout girl?" he snapped over his shoulder still whispering.

"What are you being so quiet about? There isn't anything here except us and I'm sure the only thing we'll run across probably walks on four legs and has fur all over it," she snapped back not bothering to keep her voice low. The gentle breeze stopped and an eerie silence deafened them.

"Now you've done it. If you come back here doubtin' your jus' gonna rile it. We best go on home or else we'll be sorry," Jobey turned back toward her, his face masked by shadows.

"Come on, we've come this far or are you scared," she taunted as she stepped past him.

"Damn right I'm scared and if you had half a mind you would be too. You don't want to go messin' with what you don't understand," Jobey warned as she continued.

"Come on you big chicken!" she shouted back at him.

"Uh-uh," he replied, "You go on if you want to but I'm goin' home."

"Jobey, don't be such a baby," she said as she strode back to him.

"I ain't no baby. . .I..." he trailed off and began to shake uncontrollably.

"What's the matter with you now?" she demanded staring hard at his suddenly pale face.

Darkness had enveloped them but his features shone brightly. His huge eyes were round with fear and his limbs trembled with it. A trickle of saliva slid from the side of his mouth as he stared past her.

The fine hairs on the nape of her neck began to rise as a gust of warm air blew across them. Erica turned stared in horror at what had turned Jobey into a living piece of stone.

Two large almond shaped eyes the color of red hot coals burned brightly some fifteen feet above her. The disembodied eyes floated in a sea of black as the hot wind continued to wash over her. A foul stench permeated the air as the eyes began to move closer. Her heart froze then seemed to explode with an instinctual panic born from some ancient mechanism buried deep in her brain. Her limbs felt like leaden weights dragging her toward the moldy forest floor. Somewhere inside her mind a voice screamed for her to run, to flee from this evil place where no man had tread since the first settlers.

Her body reacted purely on the need to survive; to get away. She turned and grabbed Jobey by the arm. Her legs churned as she ran through the dense stand of trees, dragging Jobey with her. He moved in jerky mechanical gyrations as she pulled him along behind her.

"Jobey get a grip and move it!" she shouted over her shoulder, knowing she wouldn't be able to continue pulling his dead weight behind her.

A sudden sharp jerk on her arm sent her sprawling on the ground, the air whooshing from her lungs. Her body ached from the tumble she had taken to the hardpacked dirt floor. Jobey's hand jerked spasmodically against her arm as she fought to catch another breath.

Struggling to her feet, she looked back to find Jobey's arm in her hand, the muscles jumping as nerves and tendons dangled freely from the socket. The blue jean material of the shirt was soaked with blood as it spurted from the appendage. A scream rose in her throat and bubbled around the bile that had already raced to her mouth. She threw the arm down and stumbled toward the skeletal tree trunks.

Her eyes blurred as she fled head first through the dead branches that stretched outward to grab her hair and clothing. Ducking past one of the oaks, she ran headlong into the huge stone monoliths that marked the passage way. Pain exploded in her chest but she fought to stay conscious and moving. A loud crashing echoed through the trees behind her as she sprinted through the trees and headed for the well-worn path that they had left not long ago.

Breaking through the line of trees, she found the moon drenched path and set off at a break neck speed as if every devil in hell were on her heels and in truth they might be. Her breathing was ragged as she crashed through the underbrush and groaned as the branches slapped at her already lacerated face. If she ever got away, she was never coming back to this place.

The hot breath was back on her neck again as she dodged past one of the last oaks toward another open meadow bathed in the shining light of the milky white moon. Sound exploded from every place as the calls of a night bird whistled over the tree tops and cicadas chirped in their nightly symphony. The wind turned chilly as a lite dew misted down from the heavens.

Erica felt her legs give way as she stumbled to her knees and knew deep in her heart that she would never make it out of this place alive. Why hadn't she listened to Jobey when he had first refused to take her to the gateway? Poor Jobey, he was dead now because of her. That thing had literally torn him to shreds.

Looking back at the tree line, she saw it standing in the shadows just inside the ring of trees. The red eyes burned like witch lamps above the upper branches, the grotesque blood red orbs shining with an evil glimmer that sliced through the blackness.

It had stopped. Her breathing was still ragged as she waited for it to advance on her. Looking around she tried to get her bearings straight, she recognized the meadow she realized with a sense of relief. In fact, she wasn't that far from the log cabin that her grandmother lived in. Had they only come this far? If she could only make it back to the house she could get inside out of the sight of this monster. Her muscles screamed as she scrambled up into a standing position. The eyes remained in their suspended state, never blinking, never moving.

Taking first one tentative step back, then another, Erica turned and ran as fast as her tired legs would allow. Diving headlong through the trees she searched wildly for any sign of a light in the cabin window to pierce the blackness of the night sky.

There in the distance she saw the faint warm glow of home. The light was a small beacon in the night that called to her, marking her way through this hellish nightmare. Time seemed to stand still as she expended the last of her energy to run through the plowed field and past the split rail fence surrounding the yard.

Collapsing on the porch, she pounded on the door as she ventured to look back toward the field. There in the watery light of an uncertain moon stood the most grotesque creature she had ever seen. Shiny skin the color of wet slate glinted wickedly at her. It stood about fifteen feet high with huge grasping claws out stretched as it advanced. Its hideous face was split by a lipless grin that revealed the razor-sharp teeth that zig zagged like a cross cut saw. Blood stained the lower half of a sharply pointed chin and dripped onto a chest cris-crossed by raised symbols too cryptic for her to understand.

Her throat constricted on a scream as she felt the hot stagnant breath fan across her face. A cold sweat broke out across her body as she screamed again and felt the blood slicked claws sink into her soft flesh.

ĦELL ĦOUNDS

Blackened silhouettes of dead tree trunks stretched like broken teeth towards the meager rays of sunlight. Twilight stole in amongst the worm rotted wood and a preternatural gloom descended on swift wings. Here in this oubliette, this place of forgetting, things that once were slowly stirred and began to breathe again.

****

"How much farther is this place?" Lilly asked as she followed the overall clad back of her cousin Feral.

"Not too far now. Mind your step the ground is getting slippery from the frost," he replied half turning to offer her a hand.

Lilly took the proffered hand and felt the rough calluses scratch against her soft skin. Feral went to the local high school but when he was home he helped his father on the farm. His calluses were nothing to be ashamed of. He was a big strapping boy with ginger colored hair and a light dusting of freckles across his cheeks. He had become Lilly's self-appointed protector when she came to live with them earlier in the summer.

Lilly couldn't remember what life had been like without Feral in it. She didn't have long to think about it as she slipped on one of the frost covered stones and reached blindly for Feral's strong hands.

"Are you sure the others will be here?" Lilly asked as Feral stood her on the rocks beside him.

He nodded but said nothing. His attention had been drawn away into the crouching specter of darkness. Lilly shivered involuntarily as her gaze drifted past his broad shoulders to the dead valley that lay spread out below their perch.

Two huge monoliths stood guard at the end of the faint trail they had been following. Their weathered sides glinted in the watery light of an uncertain moon as it began to rise through the broken tree line. No night sounds echoed through this terrible place. No wind bristled through the dead trees. Here there was only death and decay.

The heavy scent of mold wafted up from the forest floor as Feral pulled her into a small hollow between some of the sturdier tree trunks. The heat from his body warmed her and staved off the chill of night.

"Don't make a sound," Feral whispered in her ear as they continued to watch the fetid ground below their hiding place.

Lilly nodded silently and let her eyes roam through the trees searching for the others. Were they hidden like she and Feral? Did they know what was supposed to live here? Did she even believe the stories they had told her? Questions flowed freely through her mind as she searched for conformation that they were not alone in this foreboding place.

She wasn't sure what caught her attention, maybe the faint quick flash of a match being struck, but her eyes came to rest on a small cluster of dead trees directly across the path from them. She could just barely make out the dim outlines of the others. It was two more of her friends, Cara and Jim, who were both in her homeroom and had agreed to this fool's errand. They had sworn that it would be fun. Now Lilly wasn't so sure. Secretly she thought this was just an attempt by the local kids to have some fun at her expense.

Seriously, this was the modern age. Did they really think the devil had nothing better to do then appear to a bunch of stupid teenagers in the middle of the woods? The silliness of the situation crashed in on her and she opened her mouth to say so when the stench of rotten eggs made her gag. Feral tensed beside her as Lilly shut her mouth trying to block out part of the smell.

"Brimstone," he barely whispered against her ear, "it won't be long now."

Lilly felt her muscles tense at the word brimstone. She knew that was a sure sign of the devil. Could it be true? Could the stories that Cara and Jim told her be true? Lilly didn't want to admit that there may be a devil and that she had been stupid enough to want to come out to the woods and meet him. She didn't want to admit that anything could happen to them out here and no one would know but the thought wriggled in her brain like the worms that were eating away at the dead tree that pressed roughly against her cheek. She felt the first scalding tear as it escaped from her eyes and she fought hard to hold it back. She wasn't a cry baby. She wouldn't give in to this kind of fear. She just couldn't help but think what if?

Before she could bolt from their hiding place, she heard the tiny voices from farther back on the trail.

"How much farther?"

"Not much farther, just keep your voice down. We don't want to startle anything that might be sleepin'."

A giggle floated through the air from the girl that had spoken first.

"What are you gigglin' 'bout girl?" the boy must have been ten maybe twelve from the sounds of it.

"What are you being so quiet about? There isn't anything here except us and I'm sure the only thing we'll run across probably walks on four legs and has fur all over it," the girl snapped.

Lilly's eyes widened as she looked at Feral. His face had paled but he refused to move from their hiding place. Lilly's skin began to prickle and she realized that all the tiny hairs on her body were now standing at attention.

The night had become deathly silent, if that was even possible. Before it had felt dead but now it was as if they had fallen into a void.

"Come on, we've come this far or are you scared?" the girl taunted and Lilly wanted to shout for her to shut up.

"Damn right I'm scared and if you had half a mind you would be too. You don't want to go messin' with what you don't understand," the boy warned.

"Come on you big chicken!" the girl shouted.

They had just come in to view and Lilly could tell that they were daring each other out of sheer terror. The girl was goading the boy, trying to make him go farther into the valley than he wanted to go. Clearly the boy didn't wish to be there and was rethinking the wisdom of their choice.

"Uh-huh," the boy replied, "you go on if you want to but I'm going home."

"Jobey, don't be such a baby."

"I ain't no baby, I..." he trailed off and began to shake, his eyes locked on something beyond the girl's shoulder.

Lilly's gaze followed Jobey's line of sight and her heart froze in her chest. Feral's arms locked tight around her as if he could shield her from the grim visage that crashed through the broken trees on the other side of the small valley. The ground trembled and shook with each step the demon took. The foul stench of burning brimstone seemed to permeate every pore in Lilly's body.

The demon stood between the monoliths, its hairless midnight black body shined sickly beneath the moons rays. Raised symbols stood in rigid lines and swooping curly cues across it's skin. Two large almond shaped red eyes with pupils like a reptile glared down at the two young children. Talons like steel claws scraped along the monoliths sending sparks showering in a spray of painful light in the dullness of night. It was sharpening its nails.

Lilly tried to move, to make a sound, to warn the children but Feral's arms cut off her breath.

"What's the matter with you now?" the girl demanded as she stared hard at Jobey.

A trickle of saliva slid from the side of his mouth as he stared past her. The girl finally froze as if she had caught the scent of something then she slowly turned. Time stopped as she stared up in to the red glowing eyes and then she exploded in a flurry of primitive motion. Her body careened in the opposite direction as she grabbed the boy's arm and started back the way they had come. Jobey didn't react as quickly. He seemed to be in the grips of a seizure as his legs moved as if they were caught in quicksand.

As the two disappeared back down the trail, Lilly and Feral remained hidden in the broken trunks. It wasn't long before they heard the screaming. Lilly's hands shot to her ears trying to block it out. They should go and try to help the children. They should protect them, not cower in the remnants of the woods. Again, she tried to loosen Feral's grip but it was no use.

"We have to help them," she hissed.

Feral shook his head no, his eyes still glued to the valley below. Lilly turned her attention back to the dead ground and felt her stomach churn, the remains of her supper fighting to come back up.

A low thundering rumble began to roll through the woods around them. The vibrations were coming from beneath the ground and reverberating up through the soles of her feet. The overwhelming waves of sulfuric stench managed to make her supper escape through her mouth as hordes of hoary devil dogs came crashing through the tree line. They wore collars made of human skin and bone and were tethered with a long length of metal chain rusted and corroded from eons of neglect.

Behind the animals appeared a woman with hair as black as a raven's wing. Her eyes were bottomless pools and Eternity cloaked her in gossamer gowns of ebony. Her skin was as pale as cold dead flesh and her lips and fingertips were as black as the darkest night. Runic symbols adorned her barely concealed breasts and mimicked those that had been on the demon. To her left there appeared a tall man with a mane of black hair. Half his face scorched almost beyond recognition. To her right was the tormented figure of another man. His hair was greasy and unkempt.

"Deacon," Feral whispered.

Deacon...why did that name sound familiar to her? Lilly would have asked but didn't get the chance.

"Find them, devour them," the woman hissed as she let the chains fall.

The massive hell hounds bayed loudly, the sounds like a clarion call straight from Hell. In that moment of sheer panic before thought and deed became one, Lilly remembered the name

Deacon.   Deacon Drake, the boy who had gone missing.   Deacon Drake, the boy who had been rumored to have killed his girlfriend.   Deacon Drake, the boy who was now in league with the foulest creature imaginable.

There was no more time for Lilly to think about Deacon or even Cara and Jim.   Feral grabbed her hand and tugged her back through the woods veering from the trail to slip silently through the night as if they were a part of it.

Cara and Jim's screams cut through the darkness behind them.   Lilly tried to turn back to see what was happening but Feral wouldn't let her.   With a vicious tug, he pulled her ever onward toward the saving grace of home.   Her chest burned as she sucked in the dry chilly air of late autumn.   It cut through her lungs like a thousand tiny razor blades.   Her skin prickled and itchy as bare tree branches smacked her wind chapped skin drawing stinging red welts that burst with tiny droplets of blood.

The baying of the hounds was like a relentless drum beat driving them deeper into the unknown woods.   She was truly lost with no hope of finding her way out of this nightmare.   Feral continued with his unrelenting pace.   She wasn't sure if it was borne from the same terror that was tearing her mind apart or some sheer force of will that drove him on.   They broke free from the choking stand of trees and tore into a small open meadow.

Lilly stumbled and fought to regain her footing.   She stood and grabbed Feral's hand then screamed as the demon loomed behind him, sprouting from the ground. Feral turned to stare into its hateful read eyes. A sudden sharp jerk sent her sprawling back on the ground, the air whooshing from her lungs. Her body ached from the tumble she had taken to the frost frozen ground.

Feral's hand jerked spasmodically in her own as she fought to catch another breath. A warm rain began to fall. Lilly was confused until she realized the warm rain was blood spurting from Feral's lifeless body as the demon's talons slice through his muscle and bone. She stared blankly at the hand in her own then turned and threw up the last dredges of food that remained in her stomach. A scream rose in her throat and bubbled around the bile that still filled her mouth and threatened to choke the life from her.

She threw Feral's severed arm down and stumbled back toward the skeletal tree trunks. Her eyes blurred as she fled headlong into the forest. The crashing of the demon behind her was nothing compared to the thunder of her heart as she fought to find her way through the maze. She was doomed; Lilly knew this to be fact. She knew nothing about her surroundings and she no longer had Feral to see her home to safety. She was going to die in the woods and no one would ever know.

Lilly burst back out onto a path that looked familiar. She hoped against hope that it was the one they had taken earlier in the evening. Running on pure adrenalin she took the path at breakneck speed. Never once did she think of what lay at the end of it, she just knew it was the path to freedom.

As she rounded a bend in the path she found the small branch that led off to the gravel pull off where they had left their vehicles. Relief flooded her and threatened to make her legs collapse beneath her. She knew that Feral had the keys on him but Lilly knew how to hot wire a car. That was the reason she had been sent to stay with her family in William's Point. Tears streamed down her face as she skidded through the gravel to the welcome sight of Feral's sagging old 1978 Datsun king cab pickup truck.

She jerked the door open and jumped inside slamming the locks down on both doors. The baying of the hounds was a constant crashing in her ears as she fumbled with the wiring and began sparking them together. The truck protested then growled to life. Hysterical laughter bubbled up in her throat as she slammed it into gear and slewed sideways sending a shower of rocks into the mountain laurel that lined the pull off. Low growling roiled into the road behind her and red eyes lined the sides of the roadway as the hell hounds emerged from the bushes. She gunned the motor and threw up her middle finger as she made it back to the hardtop and shot down the lonely stretch of road.

Tears coursed down her face cutting tracks through the blood and gore that covered her from head to toe. Sobs of relief mixed with hiccups of hysteria as she turned on the trucks lights to keep from running off the road. She was home free, she was in the clear. She tried not to think about Feral or Cara or Jim. Too much had happened, too many people were dead. She shoved the gas pedal to the floor trying to outrun the ghosts as much as the demons that were chasing her.

The truck sputtered and bucked but complied then shot around the last curve in the road. It would be clear sailing all the way back to town all she had to do was....

The truck slammed in to the wall of hounds. They bounced and banged but didn't die. Their claws dug into the rusty metal of the truck, their jaws snapped at the windows. A scream bubbled up in her throat as she lost control of the vehicle and it careened off the road. She glanced up and in the rearview mirror saw the grim visage of Deacon Drake behind her seat. His black eyes bored into hers as his filthy fingers wrapped around her throat and strangled the life out of her.

MAD HERRIOT

Mad Herriot Higherdal lived in a stately yet aging old Victorian on the outskirts of William's Point. You could say that main street ended at her front drive with her huge house crouched there like a wicked spider waiting for innocent flies. Mad Herriot had been born and raised in William's Point and must have been as old as dirt.

She was called Mad Herriot because of her peculiarity. You see she was born in William's Point but she was never really *belonged* in William's Point. As a matter of fact, no one really understood *where* she belonged. Sometimes she was just downright odd.

Herriot Helouis Higherdal was born on a Friday 13th at 3:33 a.m. with a series of birthmarks that created a perfect star on her body. Her family was old money so even though whispers of witchery prevailed none were ever uttered in her genteel presence.

Her childhood was normal, same as all the other privileged girls of William's Point. She attended Mrs. Langley's Finishing School for girls up in Rain Canyon and had her first season just like all the other girls. Up to the time that William Maxwell began courting her, Mad Herriot had simply been Herriot; beautiful, sweet, kind Herriot.

William Maxwell was also from old money and since it was an unwritten rule that old money married old money the town thought it was a suitable match. He was a dashing young man whose parents owned several pieces of prime real estate that had been plundered by the founders from the Native Americans and jealously hoarded through the generations. After all William's Point was founded by a bunch of murderers and thieves calling themselves the righteous owners of the land.

The couple married after the proper amount of courtship time elapsed. Six years to the day after her debut, she was married in an outside ceremony in her beloved rose garden behind the newly acquired Victorian. The house had been given to her in the will of a great-grandparent as her dowry along with some river front property and a few lucrative pieces with railroad shipping access that had made her father furious, but her husband quite happy.

That was where the bliss ended. She refused to change her last name; Herriot Helouis Maxwell simply did not carry the same ring as Herriot Helouis Higherdal. Although perplexed, her husband gave in to the strange demand. No one had ever thought to besmirch their married status quite like that before but William longed for a peaceful loving marriage and asked only that the children bare the last name of Maxwell. The deal was struck and like all business arrangements, notarized and put on file at the county courthouse.

Herriot lived a happy life with her new husband in the grand old home and was the envy of all her old school friends.   She loved that the most.   She held her head high when she went to town, letting everyone know that she was better than they were.   She loved to show off her home but most of all she loved showing off her roses. If there was anything in the world she loved more than her roses no one knew what it was.   Herriot had a knack for bringing back even the deadest of rose bushes and her garden thrived under her loving care.   Herriot was very happy with her life until the night of the big storm.

William was out of town on another of his many business trips when the storm blew in. Within minutes it was a gale force that flooded the streams and washed out all the roads leading into William's Point.   Herriot was trapped in the house alone; her servants had gone into town to buy the regular supplies and visit some relatives for the day.   No one is sure when it happened but at some point, in time during the gale, Herriot had a visitor.

Now the things that are about to be told are just dark whispers and collective rumors-mind you-because it's just not polite to ask out right what exactly happened.

The day had turned to pitch as the weather forecasters sent up warnings of a hellacious storm brewing.   Lightning slashed at the sky as thunder rumbled so low it shook the foundations of the buildings.   Now Herriot was never a hot house flower - sure her hands hadn't known any arduous work but she wasn't incapable either.

She took care of all the windows and the greenhouse then pulled out the storm lanterns and extra candles. She had just settled down with a sandwich and a book when she heard a knock at the door. At first, she didn't think much about it when there were no other sounds besides that of the approaching storm. She looked out the front parlor window and saw nothing but the porch swing bumping into the side of the house.

Herriot went outside to secure the swing not wanting to have a broken window, when she saw something by the front gate. The thing by the gate must be some flotsam loosened from one of the outbuildings or possibly someone's house.

She finished securing the swing and started to go back into the house when the object began to move and not because of the wind. The thing was black as a crow's wing and had only appeared to be the size of a small dog. Now it was rising as if standing up on its back legs or shoving up through the ground. Herriot pushed the hair from her face as the thing stopped moving again. She had never been a person to fear much of anything but something about this wasn't natural.

She wavered for another moment before starting to turn to go back into the house. In that split second the thing began to unfurl. Herriot looked around for something to use as a weapon but found nothing close to hand. She took a step toward the door and the chrysalis opened a little further.

Fear seized her and she ran for the door not even daring to look back at the black object. She slammed the door behind her and slid the lock in place. Peeking out the window, she could see the cocoon completely open but the inside was bare. It teetered for a moment then blew away like a gigantic dead leaf, like one of the leaves from her rose bushes. She shook her head and figured she was losing her grip on reality, it was probably just an old tarp that had caught on the front gate and now blown on to someone else's property.

"Oh well, it's their problem now," she mumbled as she went to the front parlor to resume her book.

The rain began to spatter against the panes but within minutes it sounded like someone was dumping a washtub on the roof. Sure enough, the lights flickered and went out. No matter, she lit the lamp and adjusted the wick and continued reading.

Outside the wind hurtled anything that was not tied down at speeds near cyclone strength. It pressed the tree tops back trying in vain to make them kiss the earth. It howled like a wounded animal and raced round the chimney tops.

Herriot slammed the flue shut to keep the soot from getting on the carpet.

"Well that must be done to get rid of any dirt before the winter," she murmured in dismay at the soot that had fallen in to the bare fireplace.

The list of chores was mounting when she heard something fall upstairs. It wasn't the sound of breaking glass but more like a thud as if someone had fallen or closed one of the bedroom doors too hard. Her delicate brow furrowed, Herriot had never believed in ghost stories and she certainly didn't subscribe to the foolish non-sense most of William's Point, including her parents, believed in.

"Nonsense and drivel," she muttered as she got up and walked into the hallway to look up the staircase.

Everything was silent again but the hairs on the back of her neck seemed to sense otherwise. A chill had entered the house, one that permeated the air like a wet blanket. A shiver slunk down her spine as she went to the kitchen to light the gas stove to make a cup of tea. Yes, a nice cup of tea to chase away the damp weather.

She put the kettle on to boil and was getting out some milk and honey when she heard another knock at the door. Who would have ventured out in this kind of weather? She turned the kettle off and went to answer the door again.

A gust of wind and rain hit her full force as she held tightly to the knob and strained to see in the near darkness outside. No one there, but at the bottom of the walkway was another black object. It trembled and shook then began to rear up much the same as the last one had. Quickly she slammed the door and locked it then leaned back and gave a tiny ragged laugh.

"Hold it together girl this storm is tearing you apart at the seams," she mumbled to herself as she pushed away from the door.

Giving herself a mental shake she decided against the tea and went for a hot toddy. Forget the toddy, she'd just go straight for the bottle then sleep off this storm. She rummaged through the cabinets and found a puny little bottle that the maid kept for medicinal purposes. She took a sip and spat it out in the sink.

"You call that alcohol...." she grumbled as she headed down to the basement and then to one of the damp walls.

Pulling on one of the tools mounted on the wall she smiled as it cracked open enough for her to push the wall all the way open. She lifted one of the oil lamps higher to lead the way down the black corridor. Down here the sounds of the storm were completely blocked out. The walls were damp as she trudged through the tiny stand of running water. She had played in this place as a child. She had learned about it from her grandfather, she was the only living soul that knew about it.

The corridor opened into another room beneath the old slave quarters that now stood very empty. It had been turned into a spring house but the bars still adorned the windows. A staircase led up to the sleeping quarters where her great grandfather used to visit the females and pass many an hour with them. He had taken one in-particular as mistress and moved her into the house.

Herriot went to the farthest wall and pushed lightly on the third stone from the left. The old stones sighed as they swung open to reveal a vast room that was dusty with cobwebs. She made her way to a row of bottles and jugs and lovingly sorted through the elegant old labels.

"Ah there you are my dear," she murmured sweetly as she spied the squat brown jug that seemed so out of place.

She picked up the dust encrusted jug and wiped it off then opened it. Upending the jug just enough she tasted the strong home brew and smiled as it burned its way down her throat. Some things should never be tampered with, the recipe had been the same for over a hundred years and her child would carry on the tradition.

A warm breeze sighed across the room and touched her lightly. Herriot stopped mid-drink and peered round the semi-darkness. The breeze came again but this time it blew out the flame of the lamp. Darkness reigned, as terror seized her. This was not right. Herriot turned back to the door but found it was a wall. She gripped the jug fiercely as she tried to regain her composure.

Another sigh of warm air caressed her face as she searched the empty void that only seconds ago had been a shadowy room. At first the sounds were faint, so faint in fact they really didn't register. Far away murmurs from down a long tunnel as if time itself had been suspended. The voices were muffled as the elastic wall of space and time expanded and contracted as if indecisive about her worthiness of this gift.

A soft glow began in the center of the room then grew in slowly undulating waves as the scene unfolded. Fire light flickered and danced across sweaty cave walls as a low moan echoed in the warm womb of mother earth. A lump of flesh and bone churned in the flickering lights of those hellish flames.

Herriot held her breath as a form began to writhe in the lump. Chanting from some distance reached her ears; the witches were conjuring. Somewhere deep in her heart she knew it was the witches although no one had openly talked about them in front of her. Her attention returned to the form that was now a full grown many lying on the floor. He was not yet born, she wasn't sure how she knew it; she just did.

From the corners of the room a small blue glow began then carefully the tiny flames of the blue light danced forward. Each tiny blue flame boldly pranced forward and touched his lips. They breathed life into the magnificent male form. Seconds ticked by then the deep inhalation of breath echoed in the chamber. The chanting form outside had stopped. In one heart rending moment, his eyes opened and he was well and truly alive!

In the next second she was plunged into darkness again as the vision vanished. Panic seized her as she gripped the jug tighter and listened to the low voices that echoed in the chamber. The voices were echoes of the past, whispering down the corridors of time to her. Words of passion and pain were mixed with some sort of chanting, different than that of the witches.

"Will she live?" the hushed male voice asked in the oppressive darkness.

"I don't know sir, she's almost gone," the rusty voice answered.

"Dammit Amunda, I do not want to hear that! You must save her!" the other growled.

Silence reigned as the chanting continued, "Alright but I make no guarantees; you will not hold me responsible for the outcome. Why did you not go to the women that live in the mountains?"

"I would never take her to those hags they would steal the babe for some hellish plot."

"So instead you come to me, a black voodoo priest, poor Mr. Higher-than-All, you haven't got much choice do you," the voice sneered.

"Just save her dammit," he pleaded as the chanting stopped and silence reigned.

A scream sliced through the room and bounced off the walls as Herriot felt her blood begin to chill. Her practical side warred with the hidden superstitious side that threatened to consume her. A hot breath fanned against her neck as she turned to stare into amber eyes. They burned into her brain as she dropped the jug from her suddenly numb fingers.

"What are you doing here?!" a disembodied growl demanded.

Another shriek crashed around the room as an unearthly hand reached out and scraped along her blouse front. Terror froze her blood but adrenaline heated her up again. Herriot wheeled around and bounced off the shelves and racks as bottles rattled and tumbled to the floor, shattering into a million shards.

Herriot searched blindly for the door as the thing continued to stalk her around the room. Her hands finally found the corridor leading back to the old slave quarters. She ducked through the opening as long fingers tangled in her blouse. The sound of ripping silk was accompanied by her shriek of terror.

Herriot ran through the dark corridor convinced in her mind's eye that every demon in Hell had crawled from the Pit and was in close pursuit of her. She could almost feel their hot breath scorching her neck as she burst back into the basement. She hesitated only long enough to throw the lever that would close the door behind her.

Herriot was halfway up the stairs when she heard the loud crash against the basement wall. The tools jumped and jangled on the wall with the force of the impact. A moment of silence passed then there was another loud crash against the wall. Some of the tools shook so violently they hopped off the wall. Herriot turned and sprinted up the last of the stairs and slammed the door behind her.

The house was deathly silent. The lights flickered on once, twice; then died to blackness again. Herriot stumbled through the hallway back toward the front parlor and the lamp she had left burning there.

As she passed through the dark foyer a knock sounded at the door. Herriot's heart froze as she remembered the black thing that had trembled and grown at the gate. Again, the knock boomed into the silence; three sharp raps that seemed to squeeze the blood from her. She licked her lips and wondered what would happen if she simply refused to open the door. Silence descended for the first time since the storm had begun. She darted a nervous tongue across her lips as she inched toward the front parlor and the flickering safety of the lamp.

The house seemed to hold its breath as did Herriot as she found herself tiptoeing toward the parlor. She was just barely past the front door when the knock seemed to shatter the very air around her. It thundered in the tenuous silence of the foyer and drowned out the fury of the storm outside. Again, it sounded three times. Every nerve in her body screamed for her to continue, to ignore the knocking but she had to see who it was.

Opening the front door, Herriot braced herself for what she thought she would see. There not half a foot from her was another black object. It towered above her and trembled violently as it began to unroll. A scream tore from her throat as she slammed the door shut but not before she saw what lay inside the cocoon. His face was pale, his body long and sleek, and his eyes, those same amber eyes from the basement.

Herriot backed away from the door, slamming it shut and throwing the lock.

Stepping into the parlor she expelled the breath she had not been aware of holding. She pushed the door shut behind her and slid the bolt securely in place locking herself inside the parlor. She barely noticed the rich scent of roses that hung heavy in the air.

She could ride out the storm in the cozy little room; surely it was just overactive imagination causing her to react this way. After all, the practical Herriot that was now returning did not believe in any of this hocus-pocus bologna. Rubbing her face lightly she slid slightly trembling fingers through her hair and attempted to straighten the tangles from her otherwise perfect coiffure.

The knocking at the door had simply been another piece of flotsam pulled loose from somewhere; she would just have one of the workmen fix whatever damage had been done tomorrow. Surely, she had not seen a man; her nerves were just jangled from the fierceness of the storm; that was all. Herriot strolled farther into the room towards her comfortable seat and the sandwich that awaited her. She sat down and took a bite of the sandwich then reached for the forgotten book only to find it missing. A frown creased Herriot's fine brow. She had laid a book by the plate had she not? A look of puzzlement crossed her features then she shrugged and reached for the sandwich again.

The plate was empty. Herriot's hand grasped nothing but air. She looked at the china plate in disbelief. There had been a sandwich on it not two seconds before. She was not losing her mind there had to be a logical explanation for all this; she just had to come up with one. As Herriot looked down at the floor to see if the sandwich had slipped off the plate she heard leather creak.

Her head snapped up as she looked toward the wing backed chairs that faced the fireplace. Long slender fingers appeared around the side of one of the chairs. It was a man's hand that caressed the ancient leather with loving fingers. His nails were finely manicured and slightly long.

Herriot's eyes widened as the pale hand emerged farther and the fingers curled invitingly on the chair. Long legs stretched toward the fireplace, encased in fine black material that tapered into an expensive looking pair of black riding boots, the kind her grandfather had worn when she was a child. Herriot clutched the china plate to her chest as if it were a shield as she tried to gain a standing position on suddenly shaky legs.

"Your book is quite amusing," a soft sultry voice curled from the depths of the chair.

"Who are you?" she managed to push past suddenly dry lips.

"Come closer my pet and find out," he said with the slow sure purr of a cat.

Herriot stared at the back of the chair. Come closer he had said, hmmm not bloody likely she thought. Dropping the plate, she ran for the door. The sound of shattering china exploded in the silence of the room as Herriot grabbed the fine porcelain doorknob and yanked viciously.

The door wouldn't budge. For a moment panic seized her as she continued to fight with the door.

"There is no need to fear me, my sweet," his voice purred again.

Herriot refused to look back and searched the door for the offending object that was blocking her exit. The damn bolt, how could she have forgotten that she had slid the bolt? Jerking the slide lock back, she made a dash for the empty foyer and jerked the door closed behind her. She searched through her right pocket and produced the tiny skeleton key that would lock and unlock any door in the house. The aged metal gleamed dully in the dim light of the foyer as she inserted it in the lock and turned.

She needed to get to Maxwell's study and get the rifle he kept above the mantle. At least she would be able to protect herself. As she took a step away from the door she heard footsteps approach the other side. Another thump echoed overhead as Herriot stood in the foyer staring at the door to the parlor. From the events that had already taken place, she was not going to go upstairs to find out what was knocking around.

Outside the storm still raged. The wind ripped at the trees and tore across the mountains. The church bell rang madly, the rope having been torn free of its cleat. Inside, Herriot waited in tense expectation of what would happen next.

"Herriot..." the voice whispered from the other side of the parlor door.

"Who are you?   How did you get in here?"
she demanded.

Herriot was proud of herself, her voice had
sounded quite authoritative.

"I mean you no harm, my sweet," his voice
was a balm against the raging storm outside.

"And I'm supposed to believe that?"
Herriot didn't try to hide her skepticism.

A deep throaty chuckle rumbled from the
other side of the door and was echoed by a crash
of thunder.

"Ah my sweet, it is good that you are not
too gullible, but alas I am afraid you have already
been put into checkmate.   I have come to warn
you that your king has fallen."

Herriot's brow furrowed as she tried to
decipher that bit of cryptic nonsense.

"And what is that bit of fluff supposed to
mean?" she asked as she put her hands on her
hips and glared at the door.

She could have sworn she heard him
smile through that damn door.   Seconds ticked
by as the sounds of the rain pounding on the roof
filled the house.

"Open the door and you shall see," was
his reply.

Herriot shook her head but said nothing.
This was getting her nowhere.   Rationality had
returned and completely banished the fear and
blind terror she had felt in the basement.   This
person was real and Herriot could deal with that.

"I'm getting my husband's shotgun and
then we'll see what you have to say," Herriot said

as she turned on her heel and headed towards her husband's study.

"By all means my precious, get the gun, if it will make you feel better," his voice followed her down the hallway.

Herriot edged past the kitchen, still all too aware of the presence that had chased her through the basement. There was silence from that quarter now, a terrible pregnant silence that made the hairs at the nape of her neck stand on end. She scurried into the darkened study and fumbled for the lights. She flicked the switch and nothing happened. Just as she had anticipated, the power was still out.

There was a scrapping sound and then the pop of a match igniting made her jump a foot off the floor.

"Is this what you're looking for my dear?" his voice was liquid satin running across her raw nerves, "Shh...no need to scream and ruin the mood," he purred as she opened her mouth to do just that.

He tossed the match into the fireplace and watched as the wood caught and began to crackle.

"How fortuitous that you have such a diligent staff," he murmured as he removed the long black overcoat and draped it across the leather covered desk chair.

Herriot was arrested by his movements. Stealthy grace as if every muscle were made to be looked upon and drooled over. She was particularly interested in the tattoo that peeked out from his collar and ran up the side of his neck into his hairline.   It was the image of a rose vine complete with tiny thorns and delicate leaves.   Is she didn't know better, she could swear that she could smell the scent of the roses from her garden, clinging lightly to the air.   When had she lost her senses?   Herriot could not answer that question.   Instead of running for the gun above the mantel she was standing there like a halfwit staring at this stranger.

He moved then; not towards her, but towards the fine ivory chess set on the other side of the hearth.   His long lean fingers lovingly stroked the ivory queen as his gaze slide sideways towards her.   Herriot was frozen by the pale amber of his gaze, so familiar yet she could not place the exact shade.   His eyes were hot upon her skin but his face remained impassive.

"What did you mean when you said my king had fallen?" she managed in a tight whisper.

A smile slowly curled the corners of a mouth far too sensual for a man.   He picked up the ivory king and studied it for a moment; then motioned her to come with a beckoning finger.

Herriot moved but not of her own accord. It was as if her body were gently lifted and floated toward the dark stranger.   Her feet touched the floor once more when she was just opposite him on the other side of the hearth.   Again, the scent of fresh roses assailed her senses as he pushed a strand of long black hair behind his ear and crouched in front of the fire.   He held up the king between thumb and forefinger.   Herriot took a step forward and then crouched down as well.

"See your king as he truly is," he whispered.

Herriot stared at the ivory chess piece framed on one side by his long-tapered fingers and the flickering flames on the other side. Slowly an image began to appear. The chess piece faded and before her; in the depths of the fire an image of her husband shimmered and writhed. He was looking at her as if she were not there. Herriot's brow furrowed for a moment until she realized he was not looking at her at all but at a mirror. He splashed cologne on, the cologne he reserved for special occasions. He removed his tie and vest, and then proceeded to unbutton his shirt.

Why would he put on cologne then get undressed? she wondered.

Naked to the waist, he turned from her and walked to what must be the bathroom door. The door opened into a grand bedroom. The sounds of feminine laughter floated towards her. The image shifted and turned as if caught in the draft from the fireplace. When it stabilized her heart froze. Two bodies writhed in the bright red satin sheets. Naked flesh pressed together in wanton need as lips touched and tasted. His face was a mask of pleasure as he melded his body into the unknown enemy. Her face was blocked by his broad shoulders but her hands clasped at his back and urged him forward.

A pale lock of hair drifted across one of the pillows as the woman cried out in pleasure.

Herriot's blood boiled as her heart froze into a block of ice. Her head throbbed but she could not turn her eyes away.

The image shifted again. The lights were low but the bodies were still entwined. He was holding her as if she were a cherished possession.

"Maxwell, will we ever be together as man and wife?" the woman asked.

Herriot felt the world crumbling beneath her. It couldn't be! Indeed, it was. The bitch in heat was none other than her own baby sister. Alice, who had stood as her bridesmaid at their wedding ceremony in the rose garden, now lay embraced by her lecherous husband. Alice who was away at a boarding school, the same damn school Herriot had attended!

"Of course, my dear," he murmured into her golden hair.

"How will we do it?" Alice purred.

"She has a fondness for the homemade brew that your great-grandfather taught her to make. She doesn't know that I am aware of this weakness of hers or of the cellar she hides it in past the old slave's quarters. I've already paid a visit to the cellar and put thought to deed," he said as he stroked Alice's hair.

Herriot licked her lips as she tasted the residue of alcohol and the slight almond flavor upon her lips. Arsenic! The bastard had slipped poison into the moonshine. No wonder she had seen those things in the basement. If it hadn't been for the voice and those amber eyes....

"How long do you think it will take?" Alice pouted.

"Not long my dear. Even now there is a terrible storm raging over the town. The man at the front desk said that it had already flooded many of the rivers and streams and washed out roads. Herriot is terrified of storms. I know she is alone because I arranged for the servants to be in town. If I know her, she has already imbibed so much that she will be cold before the storm ends.

I will find her body and none will be the wiser when I call for the doctor and they see how she was drinking that god-awful concoction of hers. Then we can be together, after the appropriate time of course and you can rip out that hideous rose garden and plant whatever lovely plants you wish. Now let's not worry your pretty head any further. I have far more interesting things for you to do...." he said as his hands began to roam over her body.

The image faded one last time reverting to the reality of the stranger's hand and the chess piece.

Time slipped past; each second was a small eternity as Herriot's heart crumbled to dust. In its place, a slow anger began to build. It picked up and grew in time with the storm that crashed outside. The rain lashed at the windows as the wind ripped the shutters open.

Herriot's face seemed etched in stone as she finally turned her gaze from the chess piece to the man, a hairs breath away from her. Her eyes held all the fury of the tempest outside.

"Hell hath no fury, like a woman scorned," he whispered against her lips.

He placed the fire heated king in the palm of her hand and closed her fingers around it. "What do you require of me?" she asked, knowing instinctively that this information had a price tag attached.

A smile curled across his sensuous mouth again. His fingers slid into her hair and pulled her face to his. Again, she was assaulted by the fresh scent of roses as their lips brushed together.

"Feed the roses, my pet. You know how they love to be fed," he whispered next to her ear.

The scent of roses grew, making her dizzy with it.

"I have left a special *gift* for you upstairs, my precious. Do not fear, you will see me every evening among the leaves," he whispered as he released her hand.

The window groaned and cracked then exploded inward sending a shower of glass and rain in a maelstrom of destruction about the room. Herriot threw up her arms instinctively to protect herself as the wind howled about the room then fell to an eerie silence. When she lowered her arms the room was empty, but lying on the rug at her feet was a perfect snow-white rose in full bloom.

Herriot bent over and picked up the flower, savoring the smell of it. One of the thorns pricked her finger drawing a droplet of her own precious blood.

Sucking on the small wound she turned toward the doorway and went into the hall. She stopped in the kitchen to retrieve the axe from its place near the cook stove where they chopped kindling. She smiled as she caught sight of the open basement door and once again remembered the familiar amber eyes. A silent voice seemed to urge her on.

Quietly she padded up the stairs still clutching the rose and the king in one hand and the axe in the other. Once at the top of the stairs she hesitated only a moment as she lit an oil lamp on the table and then glided down the hallway. She stopped once to look back and although the hallway was empty she felt the comforting presence of her strange visitor.

The last room on the right a breath of air seemed to whisper against her neck.

She turned again and walked further down the hall. Herriot stopped just outside the bedroom, knowing that the mysterious thumping sounds had come from this room. Somehow her stranger had left her fallen king and his harlot of Babylon on the other side of that door. She didn't stop to question how it had happened, instead she steeled her spine and pushed the door open on silent hinges then stepped inside.

There in the middle of the large bed, swathed in red satin sheets, the couple lay eyes closed in blissful slumber. Herriot walked around the bed studying it quietly.

Where to begin, she thought.

A slow smile curved her lips as she leaned over the prone form of her husband. With a steady hand and a strength, she had not known she possessed, she drove the axe home. Two whacks and the deed was done. The second one, however, had awoken Alice who was now ashen as she stared in terror at the maniacal face of her blood-spattered sister and the transparent visage of the man behind her. His eyes burned in devilish delight as Herriot turned on her and hacked her head off as well.

Droplets of blood spattered onto the rose that had fallen to the floor and the chess piece that had landed on her husband's lifeless chest.

The flower's perfume filled the room as Herriot dropped the axe and stared at the gore before her. The satin sheets that had been slick with the couples sweat were now slick with their blood. She wrapped her sister's body in the top sheet and dragged her out of the bedroom and down the stairs. She left her by the kitchen door leading to the garden and went to retrieve her husband's body.

Opening the backdoor, Herriot breathed deeply of the air. Nothing smelled sweeter than the air after a heavy rain, nothing except her garden. The ground was pure mud, all the easier to feed the roses. The shovel tore up vast amounts of water logged soil as she planted pieces of each body in different areas of the garden. A foot here, a hand there, now her garden would grow and flourish. Herriot hummed to herself as she finished her chore and sat back to survey the job she had done. Out of the corner of her eye she saw the pale smiling visage of a man's face among the pretty blooms.

A mouth far too sensual for a man's as he blended in again, taking his place among the other blooms.

THE UNTIMELY DEMISE OF BETHEL PAGE

Bethel Page was a simple man who lived and died on the outskirts of William's Point in a small shack at the foot of the mountain. He lived an uneventful life, filled with the mundane chores of the everyday man. The only thing that set him apart was the extraordinary circumstances of his death. You see Bethel Page was a loner who stuck mostly to himself except when he needed to come into town for supplies.

He always wore faded coveralls and work boots that had seen too many winters. His hands were always covered with dirt from an honest day's labor he would say. He drove an old pickup truck with bad shocks and bald tires. It was good enough for my father and its good enough for me, he would mumble when the regulars at the feed store would ask him if he was going to trade the truck in for a newer model.

He was thin as a reed but as strong as an ox. He hadn't lived an easy life, no one could, trying to carve out a life in the rocky patch of dirt his father had won in a card game some forty odd years before. He had won it with a lousy pair of twos from a stranger with dark eyes and few words. The old man had promptly moved his young family from the urban confines of Saint Louis to the strange dark woods of the small hamlet of William's Point. It was his chance to try to be a real father and provider for his family. Old Page had always been a bit of worthless and had preferred to make his living the easy way but now he longed to try his hand at a more worthwhile pursuit.

His wife was a reformed prostitute known as wild Rosie, of course after she moved to William's Point she changed her ways and took up the gospel. She was simply known as Rose and all the good people of William's Point knew nothing of her past. She became a pillar of the church and led many crusades against the wild life that was gripping the west end of the town, namely the house of ill repute that housed some twenty prostitutes and the many taverns that were serving the devil's brew. Her crusades led to many outraged citizens and much civil unrest in the small town. All to the glory of our Lord God, she would always say.

Old Page tried hard to eke out a living for his family, but he wasn't much of a farmer. He was better at poker and running cons. It wasn't long before he went back to his old ways and began to hang out in the same places his wife was crusading against. Maybe it was a coincidence that Rose had decided to start a Holy War against these places, then again maybe it wasn't.

Many nights Bethel would lay in bed and listen to his mother praying with a fervor that would scare the devil himself. He would hide his head beneath his pillows and confess to anything just to make her stop. He tried to be a good son but sometimes something would tell him to do things and he couldn't resist. His mama would tell him it was the devil trying to lead him astray and that the only way to get rid of it was to beat the devil from him.

Bethel wasn't the only recipient of the beatings, his father often received the same treatment when he came in drunk from a night of gambling. Rose would always use the six-foot long razor strap that was folded in half then folded again to make the point. Her father had used it to discipline her when she was a child, it was the only thing the old bastard had left her when he died.

Rose would always tell Bethel the story of Cain and Abel when she had to discipline him. She would say that he had received his bad blood from the tainted past of his parents and she needed to beat it out of him, then she would make him pray with her. It was on one such night that Old Page came home drunk as usual and Rose already in a religious fervor locked him outside. "Let the devil keep you warm!" she had shouted into the freezing winter night as Old Page had trudged toward the barn.

Bethel had found his father the next morning frozen stiff, the bottle still clutched in his blue fingers. He had crawled into the barn to keep warm but had died before he could reach the stall where the livestock slept and could have shared their body heat. Old Page had died at the age of fifty-seven. He was buried quietly without much ceremony, just Bethel, a sour faced preacher, and the grave digger Ruby T. Garnett. His own mother refused to come to the funeral. Ruby offered a few words of comfort for him then chunked the old man into the clay. They had had to wait until the spring thaw so Old Page had been stored in the barn, sewn into an old sheet.

It was about that time that Bethel began to spend more time to himself than ever. His mother always chastised him and swore he was out whoring and taking up the same lifestyle that had killed his father. Nobody knew where Bethel spent his time but everyone was pretty sure that a large part of it was spent in the youngest Wynn daughter. That was understandable as she was the prettiest and deadliest of the three. One look from her melted a man's resolve and made him putty in her hands, something she enjoyed to the fullest.

Rumors of this, be it true or false, soon reached Rose's ears and an anger began to burn in her chest. Her son was no longer the good child she had tried to cultivate, he was truly the spawn of the evil her former life had led her too. You reap what you sow she would mumble when he would come home late in the night with not a word as to where he had been. She consulted the preacher as to what she should do and received a kind word and private council with him about the topic. Rose came a way a wiser woman with a goal in mind. She would cleanse

William's Point of the evil influence of the Wynn's forever.

She waited until Bethel left one night and followed him into the deep heart of the woods. There she hid in the shadows of the mighty trees as Bethel fornicated with the youngest Wynn daughter by the dancing blue flames of the bonfire while the other two danced naked beneath the full bellied harvest moon.

Hatred, red hot, boiled inside Rose as she thought of the lost child that now belonged to the devil's own wives. She removed the rifle from the folds of her cloak and took careful aim. One shot went straight through the two entwined lovers felling them at once. The other two women shrieked as they twisted with unholy agony looking for the person that had just killed their youngest sister.

Rose was still concealed in her shadowy fort, one with the forest. She took aim again and shot the other two sisters feeling the surge of triumph of good over evil. She had killed the witches that had plagued the town and brought about every evil act there.

With a satisfied smile, she turned and made her way back to the shack to pray for God's mercy on Bethel's soul. She went to bed with a clear conscience after the preacher stopped by to cleanse her sins and tell her she had done it for the good of the town. He had assured her that he would come back the next day to help her bury Bethel quietly and to get rid of the bodies of the Wynn's. Rose had fallen in to a deep dreamless sleep when she was awoken by a sound at the door.

She crept through the small shack and peeked out the window to see an empty porch. Maybe she was just hearing things. She turned from the window and went to stoke up the fire when she heard the sound again. It was a low scraping sound. Her eyes darted to the rifle that still lay on the table and then the door. She moved to the table and picked up the rifle. Never a woman to shirk from anything she marched to the door and threw it open only to find the porch still empty. As she stood in the doorway she heard the sound again.

Scrape, scrape, scrape.

The sound was familiar to her but she couldn't place it, it was more like a dim memory that she was struggling to pull to the surface. Shaking her head, she closed the door and turned back to the room. The rifle clattered from her suddenly lifeless fingers as her mouth dropped open. There sitting by the fire was Bethel and Old Page. They were sharpening a straight razor on the six-foot razor strap. Scrape, scrape, scrape.... the sound came back as the sound of her father always sharpening his straight razor too. Tears welled up in her eyes as Bethel and Old Page turned sightless eyes on her.

"This can't be happening!" she shrieked as Bethel moved toward her.

Old Page stood and looped the end of the razor strap across one of the bare beams of the ceiling. Rose turned to run outside and felt Bethel's cold hands on her shoulders as she flung open the door. Standing in the doorway were the three sisters, each with a smile that chilled her blood and behind them was a man with dark eyes and the pallor of death.

"No!!!!" she screamed as Bethel drug her backwards and held her as Old Page tied he strap around her neck.

With the straight razor in his right hand, Bethel bent and slashed her achilleas tendons in both legs, automatically bringing her down. The last thing Rose saw was the grim countenance of her father, the dark eyed stranger, as he clapped Old Page on the back with a smile. The images swirled like a heavy fog as they slowly disappeared and darkness took their place.

The next morning the good preacher and a small group of his devote followers arrived at the small shack of Bethel Page and his mother. The door stood open and inside was a small puddle of blood below an empty noose made from an age-old razor strap hung from the ceiling but Rose, ah wild Rose was nowhere to be found and neither were the Wynn's or Bethel Page.

ONE SMALL BITE

Scarlett Poe licked her ruby red lips as she watched Bran Graves from across the sea of swaying bodies. Her cool grey eyes assessed his lithe frame as it moved in time to the music with some other insignificant female. His muscles rippled beneath the soft cotton of his t-shirt and she could smell the intoxicating scent of his aftershave from her position at the bar. She could almost taste his blood as it coursed through his veins, making her mouth water. She took a drink of the spicy Bloody Mary. Yes, he would make a perfect mate. Now all she needed to do was lure him in.

Bran smiled at the luscious redhead he was dancing with. Polly something or other was her name. He had only met her ten minutes ago when Logan had shoved them together so he could get closer to her friend. Polly had chatted like a magpie about things that made no difference to Bran. He had only agreed to come to the club because Logan had harassed him in to it.

He and Logan had known each other since pre-k. They had grown up together and were closer than he ever was with his real brother Angelo. Sometimes Logan was the only person that got him. Just like tonight, Logan knew Bran had been dwelling on his last girlfriend and had made him take action. Okay so Polly what's her face might not be his cup of tea but at least it was human interaction, right? Who knew maybe he would meet Ms. Right tonight?

The song finally faded and Bran tried to think of a polite way to escape the chatty redhead. He didn't have to wonder long because Logan and his date for the night showed up and the girls went to powder their noses.

"Well bro how's it going?" Logan wagged his sandy blonde brows.

Bran didn't reply.

"Hey, you don't gotta be in love, just a little lust," Logan smiled wolfishly.

"Dude you're killing me," Bran chuckled as he punched Logan in the arm.

"Oh man that chick at the bar is eating you up with her eyes."

Scarlett watched the two men and smiled to herself. She finished the Bloody Mary and stood up as a low throbbing tribal beat blared from the speakers. She moved sensuously through the crowd of swaying bodies never losing eye contact with her prey. The insignificant female had re-emerged from the bathroom with her friend but Scarlett didn't care. There was only one thing she wanted and nothing would get in her way.

She slid up to the couple as they swayed to the music and slithered up against the redhead, sandwiching her between them. Scarlett's grey eyes bore into his pale blue ones. She danced lithely, feeling every beat of the drum as a fever pitch throbbed in her veins. She loved the wildness when it took over. She embraced the fervor and gave in to the music, abandoning herself. She mesmerized them all and in no time, she was between the redhead and her real objective.

She ground herself against him pressed her back to his chest staring at the redhead. She knew the moment the woman saw the quicksilver change in her eyes. Scarlett savored the smell of her fear. It was as intoxicating as the Bloody Mary she had consumed. She smiled as the insignificant female faltered then quickly faded in to the swaying mass of flesh surrounding them.

She turned back to her prey and nuzzled the strong pulse echoing in his neck. She would have to be careful and not maim him too much; he was far too handsome to go around with scars. Her hunger was almost insatiable but she schooled herself and inhaled his scent deeply again. She didn't want it to be over before it began.

"Want to go back to my place?" she purred in his ear.

There was a moment of hesitation before he nodded and they left the dance floor. She knew that on some darker level his body had recognized her as a predator but his mind had not accepted the fact. Just as well, it would make it easier if he didn't fight the gift she was going to give him. Scarlett led him to the black corvette coupe and slid behind the wheel. The engine purred to life as she pulled out into traffic and pointed the nose of the car out of town.

"Nice car," Bran said from the passenger seat.

"Thanks, you look good in it," she replied shifting gears and picking up speed once they left the bright lights of the town behind them.

"Aren't I supposed to be saying something like that?" Bran quipped as he slid his hand into her wild windblown black hair.

"I don't know, are you?" she smirked and took a curve a little faster than he had expected.

"Hey, we want to get there in one piece, take it easy," he murmured as he leaned in and nuzzled her neck.

Instead of slowing down, Scarlett gave the V-8 engine more gas enjoying the wildness that was now singing through her. The moon seemed to be aiding in her urgency as it stayed hidden behind a cloud bank. She could feel its call and it wouldn't be long before she had to give in. She fishtailed on to the drive leading to her house.

"What's the hurry, we have all night," Bran admonished as his hand slid down to her knee.

Scarlett pulled up to a halt in front of the rambling Tudor and turned off the car.

"We're here," she whispered before kissing Bran fully.

The heat that had already been ignited in the pit of her stomach spread as she fought for control. The urge to attack and possess was becoming unbearable.

"Let's go in," she growled as she pulled back, a predatory smile on her lips.

He either didn't notice or chose not to as he followed her through the massive oak door. The interior of the house was cool and dark, the others having already left for the evening to amuse themselves. By all rights she should be with them, instead she had to go on a different kind of hunt. They understood and they didn't fault her for it.

"This is a big house, do you live here alone," Bran asked as she led him through the massive foyer straight to a staircase.

"No, I live with my family," Scarlett tried to maintain her composure but it was turning into a losing battle.

She glanced out one of the leaded windows and saw the rays of the moon peeking from behind the cloud banks. It wouldn't be much longer before she wouldn't be able to control the change. It was going to happen and she would rather it happen in her room instead of on the stairs. She tugged him in to a fast trot as she loped down the hallway towards her suite of rooms.

They dashed through the doors into the complete blackness of her chambers as the first bars of moonlight danced down the hallway behind them. She slammed the door and shuddered as the first spasms of the change began.

"What the..." Bran stared in horror as the beauty before him twisted and contorted in pain.

Her fragile features darkened and her eyes turned to molten silver. The loud cracking of bones filled the room as she bent forward then slammed back against the door. A howl of Bran swallowed hard and sprinted to the adjoining room. He should never have come. He should have stayed in the bar with Polly. He slammed the door shut behind him and tried to shove a heavy dresser in front of the doorway.

Scarlett charged the door, the wolf now in complete control. She loved the freedom and the strength. The dresser was no match for her power as she crashed through the door and plowed into the room. He was huddled near the bed looking frantically for a weapon. She was on him in a matter of seconds.

Only a small bite, remember only a small bite, she thought as she sunk her teeth in to his shoulder.

The deed was done in a matter of seconds. She jumped onto the bed and lay watching as his body convulsed, caught in the fever of infection. He wouldn't run with her tonight or tomorrow night but he would next month and every month thereafter. He was her mate now and would be until one of them died. Her eyes glinted as the moonlight broke through the bedroom window and danced in the bloody pool on the floor beside his now pale body. He would be the alpha male of the clan and take his rightful place beside her, his alpha queen.

COMING SOON

RETURN TO WILLIAM'S POINT

The limbs of the trees clattered together like hollow bones in the dry autumn breeze. The whickering call of a night bird joined the ghostly melody as the ethereal scent of wood smoke whispered on the wind. Autumn had returned to William's Point. It had crept in on silent feet and had begun to nestle down amongst the Blue Ridge mountains.

A dense fog drifted lazily amongst the night blackened tree trunks and draped the primordial forest in its tattered spectral shroud. What strange creatures lurked in its deathly embrace? What frightening monsters of old once again roamed the land? What fiends of Hell had clawed their way towards Heaven only to be vomited up by the Earth that had once lovingly embraced them? What new freedom, strange and intoxicating, did they feel as once again they roamed the land and saw with eyes no longer dimmed by cob webs or crusted with the dusts of centuries. They were alive once more......

Author Biography

M.D. Martin was born and raised in Abingdon, Virginia. She first began writing the Legends of William's Point series in 1995 while attending Virginia Highlands Community College. She has been published in the Bristol Herald Courier Newspaper, The Sage Literary Magazine, and Treasured poems of America. One of her Christmas stories has also appeared on the WABN radio station.

When she isn't writing she is an avid reader and loves the Pendergast novels by Douglas Preston and Lincoln Child, Edgar Allen Poe, and Janet Evanovich's Stephanie Plum series. She also enjoys photography, camping, cooking, and spending time with family and friends. She currently resides in Bristol, Virginia with her two fur babies Sherlock and his sister Miss Watson.